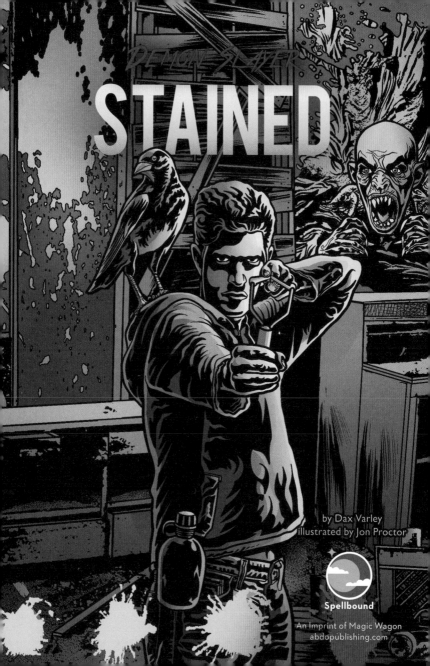

For Tracy —JP

abdopublishing.com

Published by Magic Wagon, a division of ABDO, PO Box 398166,
Minneapolis, Minnesota 55439. Copyright © 2018 by Abdo Consulting
Group, Inc. International copyrights reserved in all countries. No part
of this book may be reproduced in any form without written permission
from the publisher. Spellbound™ is a trademark and logo of Magic Wagon.

Printed in the United States of America, North Mankato, Minnesota.
052017
092017

Written by Dax Varley
Illustrated by Jon Proctor
Edited by Megan M. Gunderson
Art Directed by Candice Keimig

Publisher's Cataloging in Publication Data

Names: Varley, Dax, author. | Proctor, Jon, illustrator.
Title: Stained / by Dax Varley ; illustrated by Jon Proctor.
Description: Minneapolis, MN : Magic Wagon, 2018. | Series: Demon
    slayer ; #5
Summary: Poe leads Max to an abandoned gas station as they continue to
    search for Max's missing mom and confront demons.
Identifiers: LCCN 2016961872 | ISBN 9781532130069 (lib. bdg.) |
    ISBN 9781624029608 (ebook) | 9781624029752 (Read-to-me ebook)
Subjects: LCSH: Mothers and sons¬--Fiction. | Kidnapping--Fiction. |
    Demonology--Fiction.
Classification: DDC [Fic]--dc23
LC record available at http://lccn.loc.gov/2016961872

TABLE OF CONTENTS

CHAPTER 1
POE'S FIND 4

CHAPTER 2
MOLD & SLIME 14

CHAPTER 3
ON THE WALLS 26

CHAPTER 4
WHY HERE? 40

POE'S FIND

Poe landed on my windowsill.

He'd been out scouting for demons.

CAW! CAW!

"What's that?" I asked, taking a

frayed bit of **ribbon** from his mouth.

Wait . . . not a **ribbon**. I inspected it closer. He'd brought me back several strands of *HAIR*. Red hair. Though too orangey to be my missing *mom's*.

"Where'd you find this?" I asked.
Poe bobbed **UP** and **down**.
"Demons. **CAW!** Demons."

Yeah, I'd taught him to talk. He couldn't **YAK** about gaming or help out with my homework. But crows are **SMART**. He'd learned a few words and phrases.

I rolled the **CLUMP** of hair between my FINGERS. "Show me where you found this."

I gathered my pack of *hunting* gear. Poe led the way.

We ended up on an EMPTY road outside of town. Mostly WOODED with no houses at all. But right there in the middle of nowhere stood an old gas station—grungy and VACANT. The pumps had long ago been shut off.

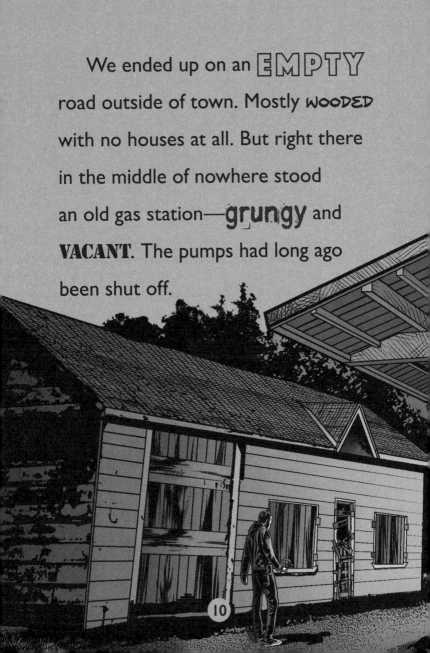

Poe *fluttered* his wings and landed on a **rusty** sign. "Demons!" he called.

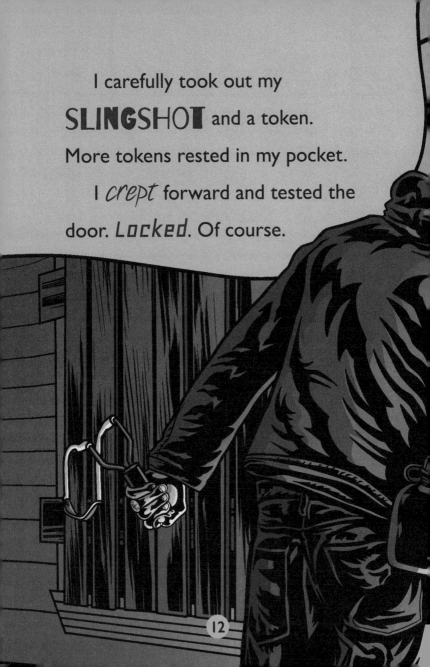

I carefully took out my

SLINGSHOT and a token.

More tokens rested in my pocket.

I *crept* forward and tested the

door. *Locked*. Of course.

MOLD & SLIME

Did I really expect this to be easy?

I peered through the large, crusted window. What a **MESS**! Sagging ceiling, crumbling floors, and **BLOTCHY** walls that looked like a case of cola **EXPLODED** on them.

But demons? None.

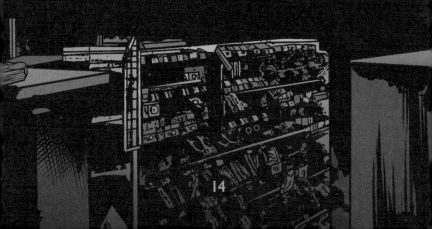

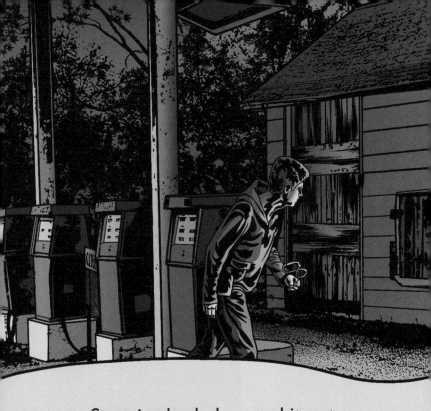

Stepping back, I scoped it out.

A place this RATTY had to be

easy to BREAK into. I walked around,

looking for a **busted** window

or a CRACKED wall.

I **CIRCLED** the whole
building. "Oh, come on," I mumbled.
"There's got to be a way in."
Poe bobbed up and down.
"CAW, CAW! CAW, CAW!" He took flight.
Ah. The way *in* was *up*.

"**CAW!**" Poe answered,
nodding his head.

"Okay."

Heading around to the side, I opened the door to the men's **restroom**. Then, placing my foot on the doorknob, I BOOSTED myself up, **GRABBED** the top of the door, and spidered my way onto the roof.

Wow! Square in the middle was a **HUGE** hole. *No wonder the ceiling droops inside.*

Poe *perched* on my shoulder. "Demons!"

"All right. Let's **GO GET 'EM**."

I lowered myself through the hole. Then, standing on a beam, I *KICKED* in the saggy part of the ceiling. It fell in large chunks. I DROPPED down to the floor.

Ew. A mixture of icky smells crawled up my nose. Stink like ROT, MOLD, and that gooey slime that sprouts on the shower curtain.

CHAPTER 3

ON THE WALLS

I turned in a full **CIRCLE**. *"Where?"* The gas station was no bigger than one of my classrooms. There was nowhere to hide.

Poe *fluttered* in front of the walls and pecked at a **splotchy** part. Soon he'd notched out a **SLOT**.

"What are you doing?"

He flew over and landed on my shoulder. "Token!" He **NIPPED** one from my hand then flew back.

The second he pushed the
token in—**BOOM!**—the splotch
EXPLODED.

"What the . . ." DEMONS!
They'd *blended* in, disguising
themselves as wall **STAINS**!

Right then, all the splotches
began to WIGGLE. I drew my
slingshot. *Whap!* Got one.

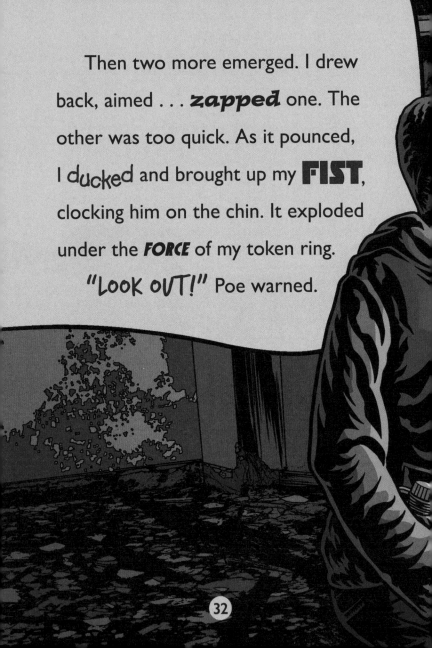

Then two more emerged. I drew back, aimed . . . *zapped* one. The other was too quick. As it pounced, I ducked and brought up my **FIST**, clocking him on the chin. It exploded under the **FORCE** of my token ring.

"**LOOK OUT!**" Poe warned.

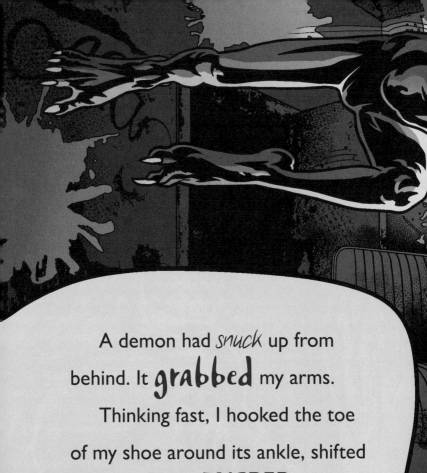

A demon had *snuck* up from behind. It **grabbed** my arms. Thinking fast, I hooked the toe of my shoe around its ankle, shifted my weight, and FLIPPED it. As it **thunked** to the ground, I loaded and fired. Right between the eyes.

But I had a problem. There were too many, coming too *FAST*. I went at them with both fists. **Punch!** Whap! **Punch!** Whap! **Punch!** Whap! Demon dust clouded the air.

Poe DIVE-BOMBED as many as he could. They CLAWED at him, causing feathers to *fly*.

One **HEFTY** demon landed on my back. My knees **buckled**, but I stayed upright. Still, it had me PINNED. It kept a hard grip on my crossed wrists.

I tried to tug free. No go. It sank its RAZOR teeth into my neck. "AOOWWWWW!"

CHAPTER 4

WHY HERE?

Pain screamed through me as  warmed the collar of my shirt. I had a token **CLUTCHED** in my hand. But there was no way to press it to the monster's **flesh**.

"Poe!" I shouted. I FLIPPED
the token with my thumb, like
someone calling heads or tails.
Poe *caught* it in midair.

Swooping down, Poe **BULLETED**

straight into the demon. Then—

WHOOSH!—he came out

through its dust on the other side.

With my **SLINGSHOT** drawn,
I *jerked* in all directions.
No more demons. The only
BLOTCHES left looked old
and natural.

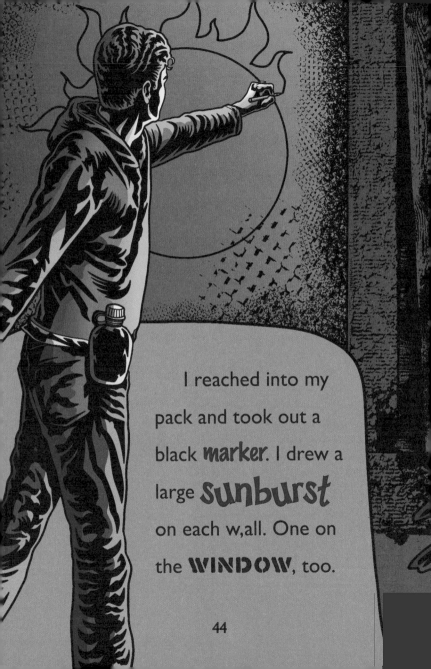

I reached into my
pack and took out a
black **marker**. I drew a
large **sunburst**
on each w,all. One on
the **WINDOW**, too.

44

"Attaboy," Poe said.

"Yeah. That'll keep them **OUT**."

Yet still I wondered why Poe had found ginger HAIR here.

Once outside, I sat down by the old pumps. "I don't get it. Why here?"

"Here," Poe echoed.

That's when I saw it. Something caught in a BUSH. "No. Way."

My heart thumped as I went over and plucked up a scrap of cloth. It was FILTHY and FADED. But I recognized it right away. It was from *Mom's* nightgown.

I **CLUTCHED** it in my shaky hand and glanced off at the **DEEP** woods. Mom *had* been here. Here. Why? And where in the world was she now?